Unicorn Princesses
PRISM'S PAINT

Unicorn Princesses

PRISM'S PAINT

Emily Bliss

illustrated by Sydney Hanson

BLOOMSBURY

NEW YORK   LONDON   OXFORD   NEW DELHI   SYDNEY

First published in the United States of America in December 2017
by Bloomsbury Children's Books
www.bloomsbury.com

Bloomsbury is a registered trademark of Bloomsbury Publishing Plc

For information about permission to reproduce selections from this book, write to
Permissions, Bloomsbury Children's Books, 1385 Broadway, New York, NY 10018
Bloomsbury books may be purchased for business or promotional use.
For information on bulk purchases please contact Macmillan Corporate and
Premium Sales Department at specialmarkets@macmillan.com

Library of Congress Cataloging-in-Publication Data
Names: Bliss, Emily, author. | Hanson, Sydney, illustrator.
Title: Prism's paint / by Emily Bliss ; illustrated by Sydney Hanson.
Description: New York : Bloomsbury, 2017. | Series: Unicorn princesses ; 4
Summary: After one of Ernest the wizard-lizard's spells goes awry, draining color
from Princess Prism and her domain, the unicorn princesses call on the human
girl Cressida to help Prism locate the Valley of Light's missing rainbow so she can
regain her magic and repaint the land and creatures.
Identifiers: LCCN 2017010911 (print) | LCCN 2017033153 (e-book)
ISBN 978-1-68119-338-0 (paperback) • ISBN 978-1-68119-337-3 (hardcover)
ISBN 978-1-68119-339-7 (e-book)
Subjects: | CYAC: Color—Fiction. | Lost and found possessions—Fiction. |
Unicorns—Fiction. | Princesses—Fiction. | Magic—Fiction. | Fantasy.
Classification: LCC PZ7.1.B633 Pr 2017 (print) | LCC PZ7.1.B633 (e-book) |
DDC [Fic]—dc23
LC record available at https://lccn.loc.gov/2017010911

Book design by Jessie Gang
Typeset by Westchester Publishing Services
Printed and bound in the U.S.A. by Berryville Graphics Inc., Berryville, Virginia
2 4 6 8 10 9 7 5 3 1 (paperback)
2 4 6 8 10 9 7 5 3 1 (hardcover)

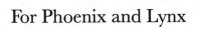
For Phoenix and Lynx

Unicorn Princesses
PRISM'S PAINT

Chapter One

In the top tower of Spiral Palace, Ernest, a wizard-lizard, scratched his long nose. He straightened his pointy purple hat and his matching cape. He picked up his magic wand. And he gazed down at a gray slug staring up at him from the tabletop. She twittered her long antennae. "I've been dreaming of this moment for months," she said. "Thank you so much for helping me!"

Ernest grinned. "It's my pleasure," he said. "And besides, I've been looking for excuses to practice my color-changing spells." He cleared his throat. He lifted his wand above his head. And then he stopped. "Um," he said, blushing, "could you remind me one more time what color you want to be?"

The slug smiled. "Ever since I was a tiny girl slug, I've longed to be the color of green grass. I'm tired of looking like a storm cloud."

"I've got to admit, it is awfully nice being green," Ernest said, looking down at his scaly, green hands. "And I've got just the right spell." He raised his wand again. But then he paused and his cheeks turned an even deeper shade of pink. "Oh dear, I've already forgotten your name. Could you tell me, just one last time?"

The slug rolled her eyes. "Sally," she said. "Sally the Slug."

"Oh yes, of course. That's right," Ernest said. "Now I'm ready." He took a deep breath. And he waved his wand as he chanted, "Sluggadug Swiggadug Sludgerug Slass! Make the Valley as Clear as Glass."

Ernest stared at the slug and waited. But her head, tail, and antennae remained gray as ever. He furrowed his brow. "Now, why didn't that work?" he asked.

"First of all," the slug said, frowning, "My name is *Sally*, not *Valley*. And second of all, you said, 'Clear as glass,' not, 'Green as grass.'"

Ernest slapped his palm against his forehead and groaned, "Oh dear!"

Just then, thunder rumbled and six bolts of silver lightning tore across the sky. The wizard-lizard rushed to the window and looked outside to see shimmering ribbons of red, orange, yellow, green, blue, and purple rising out of a valley in the distance. Soon, the streams of color formed a rainbow.

More thunder boomed. The rainbow flashed and glittered. And then, with a final bolt of lightning, the rainbow soared high

into the sky, flipped three times, and plunged downward.

"Oh dear!" Ernest exclaimed as he raced over to his bookshelf. He pulled out several thick, dusty books, looked at their covers, and tossed them across the room. Finally, he found a tiny, red book entitled *Undoing Color Spells*. He scanned the table of contents and flipped to the last page. He read out loud, "To reverse a spell that has drained the color from any part of the Rainbow Realm, find the missing rainbow and use it to repaint the land and creatures."

Still clutching the book, Ernest rushed out of his room and down the stairs, shouting, "The missing rainbow! We need to find the missing rainbow!"

Sally sighed and shrugged. She blinked her slate-colored eyes and twittered her antennae. "I guess I'll just have to keep being gray for now," she said. And with that, she glided off Ernest's table, leaving a shiny trail in her wake.

Chapter Two

Cressida Jenkins followed her older brother, Corey, off the yellow school bus. As soon as his feet hit the ground, Corey raced toward their house. Cressida knew he was in a hurry to play soccer with his friends before he started his homework.

As the bus pulled away, Cressida waved to her friends, Daphne, Eleanor, Owen, and Gillian. They waved back through the bus window, and Gillian shouted, "See you tomorrow, Cressida!"

"See you tomorrow!" Cressida called back. The bus rolled down a hill and disappeared around a corner. Cressida closed her eyes and took a deep breath. She listened to the birds chirping, and smiled as she felt the bright afternoon sun on her head and shoulders. Then, with a grin on her face, she skipped toward her family's house carrying her backpack and four rolled-up pictures she had painted in art class that day. Each was a portrait of one of the unicorns she had met in the Rainbow Realm—a magical world ruled by seven princess unicorns. In one painting, yellow Princess Sunbeam danced among the purple cacti in the Glitter Canyon. In another, silver Princess Flash raced up the Thunder Peaks. A third painting showed green Princess Bloom eating roinkle-berries in the Enchanted Garden. And in the fourth, which she had finished only a few seconds before art class ended, purple Princess Prism posed in front of Spiral Palace, the unicorns' home. She had wanted to paint the other three unicorns—orange Princess Firefly, black Princess Moon, and blue Princess Breeze—but she had run out of time.

"How creative! What a vivid imagination you have," Ms. Carter, her art teacher, had said as she looked at Cressida's paintings.

"Thank you," Cressida replied. She knew better than to tell Ms. Carter, or any other adult, about her trips to the Rainbow Realm. None of the adults she knew even believed in unicorns. They most certainly wouldn't believe Cressida could visit the Rainbow Realm at any time by pushing a special key into a tiny hole in the trunk of an oak tree in the woods behind her house.

Cressida skipped past her neighbors' houses, up her driveway, and along the walkway that led to her family's brick house. All the while, her silver unicorn sneakers' pink lights blinked and flashed. "I'm home!" she called out, as she opened the gray front door.

"Hi, honey!" her mother called from the

living room. Her mother worked from home, and Cressida could hear the sound of typing on the computer.

Cressida carried her backpack and her unicorn paintings into her bedroom and placed them on her bed. In just a few minutes, she planned to start her math homework—a page of long division problems she felt excited to solve. But first, she decided to hang up her paintings. She grabbed a small jar of thumbtacks from her desk. Next, standing on her tiptoes on her desk chair, she tacked each unicorn portrait to her bedroom wall. After she finished, she sat on her bed and thought about her unicorn friends.

Just as Cressida turned to pull her math

folder from her backpack, she heard a high, tinkling noise, like someone playing a triangle. Her heart skipped a beat. She leaped over to her bedside table and opened the drawer. Inside, she found the old-fashioned key the unicorn princesses had given her. Its crystal ball handle pulsed and glowed bright pink—it was the signal the unicorns used to invite her to the Rainbow Realm.

Cressida shoved the key into the pocket of her orange corduroy pants and straightened her yellow T-shirt, which had a glittery picture of a rainbow-striped cat on the front. Then she dashed out of her room, down the hall, and to the kitchen, where she grabbed an apple. "I'm going for a quick walk in the woods!" Cressida called out to her mother. Fortunately, time in the human world froze while Cressida was in the Rainbow Realm, meaning that even if she spent hours with the unicorns, her mother would think she had been gone only a few minutes.

"Have fun, sweetheart," her mother said amid a flurry of typing.

Cressida ran out the back door, through her backyard, and into the woods. As she hurried along the trail that led to the giant oak tree with the magic keyhole, she ate her apple and wondered what the princess unicorns were doing that afternoon. She couldn't wait to see her magical friends, and to tell them all about the pictures she had painted.

But just before she reached the oak tree, Cressida stopped short.

Standing by the tree's trunk stood a unicorn Cressida didn't recognize. The unicorn looked as though she were made of colorless glass. Around her neck hung a ribbon, also clear, with a pendant that looked like a large crystal. In her visits to the Rainbow Realm, Cressida had never met a clear unicorn. And the other unicorns hadn't mentioned another sister.

For a moment, Cressida watched the unicorn, who was frowning as she stared at her transparent hooves.

"Hello," Cressida said, smiling.

The unicorn looked up, startled. Then her eyes lit up with relief. "Cressida! I thought you'd never get here!" the unicorn exclaimed. "We've been calling you all day. I got tired of waiting and decided to come find you."

The unicorn's voice sounded familiar to Cressida, but she couldn't imagine how she might have forgotten meeting a clear unicorn. "Have we met before?" she asked, feeling a little rude.

For a second, the unicorn looked hurt and confused. And then she laughed. "Of course you don't recognize me! I'm clear!" she exclaimed. "It's me, Princess Prism."

"Prism!" Cressida said, rushing over and wrapping her arms around the unicorn's neck. She expected Prism to feel hard and cold, like glass, but instead Prism felt warm and soft. "What happened?"

"Well," Prism began, "Ernest was casting spells this morning, and he accidentally drained all the color from me and my domain, the Valley of Light. And my magic amethyst isn't working the right way."

Prism glanced down at the clear stone on her ribbon necklace. All the unicorn princesses had gemstones that gave them unique powers. Prism usually wore a purple amethyst on a green ribbon that allowed her to turn objects any of the colors of the rainbow.

"Watch what happens when I try to use my magic," Prism said. She pointed her horn at Cressida's silver sneakers. The glass-like stone shimmered, and glittery light shot from her horn. Immediately, the sneakers turned clear, so both she and Prism could see Cressida was wearing one orange sock and one pink sock.

Cressida wiggled her toes and giggled. "I guess I should have worn matching socks today," she said.

"If my magic were working, I could fix that for you," Prism said, smiling. But then her face fell. "The worst part about my magic being broken is I can't make art. I've had exactly thirteen ideas for pictures today since my magic broke, and I haven't been able to paint a single one. It's terrible! Every time I've tried to paint, I've accidentally turned something clear."

Cressida nodded sympathetically. Often, while she was riding in the car or sitting at her school desk, she had ideas for stories she wanted to write and pictures she wanted to draw. She didn't like having to wait until later to start her creative projects, either.

"The only way to reverse Ernest's spell is to find the Valley of Light's missing rainbow and use it to repaint my domain," Prism explained. "You're so good at finding things and solving problems that I thought you could help me. So, will you? Please!"

"Of course!" Cressida said.

"Fantastic!" Prism said, turning toward the giant oak tree. "By the way," she said, kneeling as Cressida climbed onto her back, "where were you all day? We've been calling you for hours!"

"School, of course," Cressida said, gripping Prism's clear mane.

"School?" Prism replied, sounding confused. "What on earth is that?"

Cressida smiled. "It's where human girls and boys go all day to learn things. Like math and science and reading and history."

"Huh," said Prism. "I've never heard of that." She used her hoof to riffle through a pile of leaves at the base of the oak tree. "Now, where did I leave my key? Aha, here it is." She used her mouth to pick up an old-fashioned silver key with a crystal ball handle—just like the one Cressida still had in her pocket. The unicorn pushed the key into a hole at the base of the tree. Suddenly, the woods began to spin, so that first they looked like a blur of brown and green before everything went pitch black. Then, Cressida felt as though they were falling through space, and she held on tightly to Prism's mane.

With a gentle *thud*, Cressida and Prism landed in the front hall of Spiral Palace. At first, the room looked like a dizzying swirl of white, silver, pink, and purple. But soon enough, the spinning room slowed to a stop. Cressida grinned to see Sunbeam, Flash, Bloom, Breeze, Moon, and Firefly all lounging on large pink and purple velvet couches.

Chapter Three

The unicorn princesses leaped over to Cressida and Prism. Their magic gemstones glittered in the light of the palace's chandeliers, and their hooves clattered against the shiny, marble floors.

"Cressida!" Sunbeam exclaimed, dancing in circles on her gold hooves. "My human girl is back!"

"I told you she'd come," Bloom said, winking at Cressida and smiling reassuringly at Prism.

"We're so glad you're here!" Flash said, rearing up.

"Now that Cressida's here, it'll be no time before you can paint more pictures," Breeze said. "Sunbeam and I will even come help you look for the missing rainbow."

Firefly and Moon smiled at Cressida and flicked their manes and tails.

"You wouldn't believe how impatient Prism was getting," Sunbeam said. "After we called for you to come this morning, she paced the front hall for two hours. Then she insisted on going to the human world to find you."

"Cressida said she was at a place called 'school' all day and that's why she couldn't come earlier," Prism said. "Have any of you ever heard of that?"

The other unicorns furrowed their brows and shook their heads.

"Apparently, it's where human girls and boys go to learn things," Prism said.

Cressida giggled. "School is pretty fun," she said. "In my art class today, I painted pictures of Sunbeam, Flash, Bloom, and Prism. Next week, I'm going to paint Breeze, Firefly, and Moon."

Prism's eyes widened. "You get to paint at school? And you painted a picture of me? I want to go to school!" Prism exclaimed.

"Maybe sometime you can come with

me," Cressida said, excited at the thought of bringing a unicorn with her to school. Only humans who believed in unicorns were able to see them, and she wondered if any of the students in her class would even know Prism was there. She was certain none of the teachers would have any idea.

"Anyway," Flash said, smiling and rolling her eyes at Prism, "thank you so much for coming, Cressida. I know Prism is eager to get her magical powers back so she can paint. She's been moping around the palace all day and accidentally turning our furniture clear."

Cressida noticed two clear armchairs

and a clear couch on the far side of the room. "I'm excited to help," she said.

"Well," said Prism, swishing her tail, "are you ready to go?"

"Absolutely!" Cressida said. Just as she was about to climb on Prism's back, she heard rapid footsteps in the hallway that led to the palace's front room.

"Wait! Wait! Oh dear! Oh dear!" a high voice called out. Cressida smiled. She would recognize that voice anywhere: it was Ernest, the wizard-lizard.

"Cressida!" Ernest exclaimed, rushing toward her and trying to catch his breath, "before you go search for the missing rainbow, I wanted to give you a present."

"Uh oh," Bloom whispered, "Ernest is about to try to do even more magic."

"I heard that!" Ernest said, but then he smiled. "You're right that magic hasn't been going that well for me today."

"Just today?" Flash teased.

"Well," Ernest said, "it's true that occasionally my spells don't work out."

"Only occasionally?" Sunbeam said, winking.

Ernest rolled his eyes and cleared his throat. "I'm sure I can do this spell perfectly. I've been practicing all day."

"We're just kidding with you, Ernest," Breeze said. "We appreciate all your hard work."

Ernest grinned and took a deep breath.

He pulled his silver wand out of his cape pocket, raised it, and chanted, "Paintily Smaintily Colorfully Foo! Make a Rainbow Hawk and a Quaint Thrush, Too!"

Wind swirled around Cressida, blowing her dark hair into her face. And then, on the marble floor in front of her sat two birds, both blinking and looking confused. One was a large hawk with feathers that were every color of the rainbow. The other

was a smaller bird Cressida didn't recognize, wearing an old-fashioned black top hat and a little black coat. He carried a wooden walking stick.

"Oh dear!" Ernest mumbled, scratching his forehead. "Not again!"

Cressida giggled. The hawk was the most beautiful and colorful bird she had ever seen, even prettier than a peacock. "What are you looking at?" the hawk said haughtily. "Haven't you ever seen a rainbow hawk?" Then, he spread his wings, flew up to the ceiling, and perched on a chandelier. Cressida smiled and shrugged.

She looked down at the smaller bird. "Who are you?" she asked.

"Pleased to make your acquaintance,"

the bird said, bowing and tipping his top hat. Cressida noticed he had a speckled chest. "I'm a quaint thrush."

"What does that mean?" Cressida asked.

"Well," the bird said. "Quaint means a combination of cute and old-fashioned. And a thrush is a songbird." With that, the bird chirped a song that sounded like the kind of music people listened to long before there were computers, televisions, or even radios.

"Well, it's wonderful to meet you, rainbow hawk and quaint thrush," Cressida said, glancing up at the chandelier and then down at the floor.

"Oh dear! Let me try again!" Ernest said. He took a deep breath, waved his wand, and chanted, "Paintily Smaintily Colorfully Foo! Off with the Hawk and the Thrush to the Zoo! Make a Rainbow Smock and a Paintbrush, Too!"

Another gust of wind swirled around Cressida, and the hawk and the thrush disappeared. When she looked down, Cressida was wearing an art smock with a huge rainbow across the front. In its pocket was a long, clear paintbrush with soft bristles. "Perfect!" Ernest exclaimed. "I told you I could do it!"

"Thank you," Cressida said, admiring the smock and touching the soft bristles on the paintbrush. She couldn't wait to use it. "Thank you, Ernest! This is absolutely perfect," she said. "And it was also pretty

fun to meet the rainbow hawk and the quaint thrush."

"Of course!" Ernest said. He pulled a watch on a long chain out of his cape pocket and groaned. "Oh dear! I was supposed to meet Ally—or was it Cally?— fifteen minutes ago to try again to turn her blue. Or was it purple? Oh dear!" He turned and sprinted off, calling out, "Good luck, Cressida!"

Prism and the other unicorns smiled affectionately as they watched Ernest disappear down the hall. Then Prism looked at Cressida, "Now that you have your smock and your paintbrush, are you ready to come with me to the Valley of Light?"

"Absolutely," Cressida said.

"And you'll come help look, too?" Prism asked, glancing at Breeze and Sunbeam.

"Of course!" Breeze said. "I promised Sunbeam I'd teach her how to fly a kite this afternoon, but after that we'll come right over."

"Thank you!" Prism said. Then she kneeled down, and Cressida climbed onto Prism's clear back.

"I can't wait to paint again!" Prism called out as she trotted toward the palace's front door. Cressida felt a jolt of nervousness: she thought she would be able to find the missing rainbow, but she wasn't completely sure. She took a deep breath. All she could do was her best, she reminded herself.

Chapter Four

Outside Spiral Palace, Prism trotted along the clear stone path that led from the castle into the surrounding forest. For a moment, as she held onto Prism's mane, Cressida turned her head back toward the sparkling, white palace, shaped like a unicorn horn. It looked beautiful in the bright afternoon sun.

"I'm excited to see the Valley of Light," Cressida said, facing forward again.

"I can't wait to show it to you," Prism said, turning onto a narrow path that cut through a cluster of pine trees. "Even though it looks awfully strange right now."

Just then, they passed a meadow full of dandelions and buttercups. Prism slowed down. And then she stopped. "You mentioned you painted pictures of my sisters and me in . . ." Prism's voice trailed off. "What did you call it? Art snass?"

Cressida giggled. "Art class," she said.

"Does that mean," Prism asked, sounding excited, "that you like to paint?"

"I love painting!" Cressida said. "And I also like making things out of clay."

"Me too!" Prism said. "Well, I love painting! Clay is pretty tough to work with if you have hooves. Everything I try to make just turns out as flat as a pancake."

Cressida giggled.

"Anyway," Prism continued, "even though I'm desperate to fix my magic powers so I can paint again, there's something I've always wanted to do. And given that I'm clear at the moment, and that you love to paint, there won't ever be a better time. Are you ready for a little art adventure before we find the missing rainbow?"

"Absolutely!" Cressida said.

"Fantastic," Prism said, kneeling down. "It might be better if you walked, since getting to the village is a little tricky."

"The village?" Cressida asked, sliding off the unicorn's back.

Prism smiled mysteriously. "Follow me!" she said, and she flicked her mane and turned off the path and into the sea of yellow flowers.

As Cressida walked alongside Prism, she picked dandelions and wove together

two wreaths. She placed one on Prism's head and the other on her own.

"Thank you!" Prism said. "I've also always wanted to make a dandelion crown, but that's another thing that's impossible to do with hooves."

Cressida and Prism came to the edge of the meadow. "This way!" Prism said, taking a sharp turn down a steep hill dotted with thorny bushes. Cressida followed her, holding her arms out to her sides for balance as she hiked. Soon, they came to an even steeper hill, covered in shiny, green moss. "There's only one way to go down!" Prism declared as she sat on her hind legs, scooted to the edge of the hill, and glided down it. "Wheeeee!" she called out before she landed in a bed of pine needles at the bottom.

A slick, mossy hill seemed like the best slide Cressida could imagine. She sat down at the top of the hill and pushed herself forward. "Wheeeee!" she yelled, going much faster than she had ever gone on any playground slide. When she landed in the pine needles at the bottom, Cressida looked in front of her and sucked in her breath. Before them was a clearing filled with miniature houses made of moss, bark, twigs, leaves, and stones. Each house was painted in the most vibrant colors Cressida could imagine: magenta, robin's egg blue, lime green, fuchsia, teal, violet, and scarlet.

"Who lives here?" Cressida asked,

suddenly wishing her parents would paint their brick house—or even just their gray front door—one of the colors she saw here.

"You'll see," Prism whispered. "Do you like the colors of the houses? I used my magic to paint them myself!"

"I love them," Cressida replied.

Prism grinned and called out, "It's Princess Prism! Is anyone home?"

Cressida heard rustling noises. Soon, the houses' front doors opened, and out stepped creatures that looked like tiny girls with wings. They were, Cressida realized as her heart skipped a beat, fairies.

The fairies were even more colorful than their houses. One with turquoise skin, pink hair, and magenta wings straightened her orange dress. Another, with green skin, purple hair, and a white dress beat her red wings as she did a somersault in the air. More and more fairies, all with different colors of skin, hair, dresses, and wings stepped outside. Several jumped up into the air and hovered, beating their wings.

Just then, a fairy with dark blue skin, clover-colored hair, a lavender dress, and gold wings fluttered over to Cressida and Prism. As she got closer, Cressida noticed she wore a wreath made of daisies, violets, and roses. "Princess Prism!" the fairy called out. "I heard all about what happened with Ernest! I must say, you do look lovely even when you're completely clear. And what a beautiful dandelion crown you have."

"Well, thank you," Prism said, laughing. "Cressida, this is Titania, Queen of the Painted Fairies. And Titania, this is Cressida, our favorite human girl who has come to help find the missing rainbow."

"Hello, Cressida," Titania said.

"It's a pleasure to meet you," Cressida replied.

The fairy fluttered her wings. "I sure hope you can find the rainbow! Do you need help looking?"

"Thank you," said Prism. "I think we're in good hands with Cressida. Right now, I'm wondering if we could use some of your paint. We want to have a little fun before we start searching." Prism winked at Titania.

"I bet I know exactly what you want to do!" Titania said. "Luckily, my paint is already out and ready to use, since I was just painting my hair. It was lavender before, and I just changed it this afternoon. What do you think?" She twirled around so they could admire her long green curls. "I get bored if I don't paint it a new color at least twice a week."

"I love it!" Prism said.

"Me too," Cressida added, nodding.

Titania turned back toward them. "I'll go get the paint. And then the other fairies and I are going to start building a palace for ourselves out of pebbles." She looked at Prism. "When we finish, we're hoping you'll come paint it for us, provided you have your magic back."

"Of course!" Prism said.

Titania turned and flew inside a scarlet house with a bright pink roof and an orange door. A few seconds later she reappeared with a tray of metal cups, each filled with a different color of paint. "The paint is magic," Titania explained, handing the tray to Cressida. "It dries instantly. And instead of dipping your brush in water to clean it off, just tap it twice."

"Thank you so very much," Cressida and Prism said.

"My pleasure," Titania said. "Now I

need to go help the other fairies stack pebbles. When we're finished with our palace, it will look like a giant wing." Just before Titania turned and fluttered away, she said, "And please do let us know if we can help you later."

Chapter Five

Prism looked at Cressida and smiled nervously. "My sisters make fun of me when I say this, but I get tired of *always* being purple. And since I'm clear today, I was thinking that maybe you could, well—" Prism, embarrassed, looked down at her hooves.

"Do you want me to paint you?" Cressida

asked, so excited she couldn't help but jump up and down.

"Well," Prism said, "um, yes, if you wouldn't mind."

"I'd love to!" Cressida said. She looked down at her rainbow smock and pulled the paintbrush from the front pocket. As soon as she wrapped her hand around it, it hummed and glowed. She felt as though she were holding a magic wand. "What color would you like me to start with?" she asked.

"I have to admit, I've always wanted a pink stripe on my nose," Prism said.

Cressida gently lifted the dandelion crown from Prism's head and laid it on a nearby rock. She dipped the brush's bristles into a cup of bright pink paint, and the brush made a flutelike sound. Cressida smiled and painted a pink stripe from Prism's horn down to her nose.

"That tickles!" Prism said, twitching her nose at the feeling of the bristles. "How does it look?"

"Fantastic!" Cressida said. She tapped the brush twice with her other hand, and immediately, the pink paint disappeared from the bristles. "What color should I use next?"

"You decide," Prism said. "After all, you're the artist."

Cressida looked at the paints for several seconds, and then dipped the brush into a cup of fluorescent green paint. This time, the brush made a sound like a trumpet flourish. Cressida painted one side of Prism's head, including her ear, green. Next, she tapped the brush twice, dipped it into a cup of violet paint, and listened as it clanged like a bell. She painted the other side of Prism's head violet. Soon, Cressida had painted Prism's front legs orange, her hind legs ruby red, her back teal, her belly magenta, all four hooves canary yellow, and her mane and tail black.

"How do I look?" Prism asked, grinning and swishing her tail.

"Wonderfully colorful," Cressida said. "But you need some finishing touches!" She painted the ribbon around Prism's neck maroon and the glass-like amethyst mint

green. With peacock-blue and emerald-green paint, she decorated Prism's body with stars and hearts. And finally, she painted rainbow stripes all the way up Prism's horn. "All done!" Cressida said, beaming proudly as she looked at Prism.

"I can't wait to see it," Prism said, and she galloped to a nearby puddle. As soon as she leaned forward and saw her reflection, she whinnied with delight. "Oh, I love it! Cressida, I wish you could paint me different colors every day! This is so much more fun than just being purple all the time. Thank you!"

"That was the most fun painting I've ever had," Cressida said.

"Wow! What an amazing paint job," a

voice called out from behind Cressida and Prism. Cressida turned and saw Titania fluttering in the air. "Cressida, we'll have to invite you back to the Rainbow Realm to paint our palace once we finish building it!"

"I thought you said I could do that," Prism said, looking jealous of the attention Cressida was getting for her artwork.

Titania smiled reassuringly at Prism. "The palace will be big enough that you can both help paint it," she said.

Prism sighed with relief. "Thank you so much for letting us use your paint," the unicorn said. "And now, I think Cressida and I better go find the missing rainbow."

"See you soon!" Titania said. Before she fluttered away, she picked up Prism's dandelion wreath and put it back on the unicorn's head. "I wouldn't want you to forget your crown. You are a princess, after all," the fairy said.

"Thank you," Prism said. Then, she kneeled down and said, "Climb aboard! I know a short cut to the Valley of Light from here."

Swinging her leg over Prism's back and grabbing onto the unicorn's newly black mane, Cressida said, "Let's go find the rainbow!"

Prism galloped downhill for several minutes, weaving through patches of gigantic ferns and groves of pine trees. Then she stopped and said, "We're almost to the Valley of Light. Close your eyes!"

Cressida shut her eyes as tightly as she could. She felt Prism turn and then take several steps forward.

"Okay!" Prism called out. "You can look now!"

Chapter Six

Cressida opened her eyes and blinked in astonishment. Before her lay a valley in which everything was colorless and see-through. Diamond-like daffodils and tulips poked up from grass that looked like icicles. A gurgling river rushed and swirled down a bed of rocks that looked like giant crystals, as clear fish jumped in and out of the

rapids. Over the river arched a bridge that looked like it was made of ice. Nearby, trees with glass-like branches and clear leaves swayed in the breeze. Squirrels, chipmunks, and rabbits, all of which looked like glass animal figurines, played by the riverbank and chased each other through the grass.

"Wow!" Cressida said, inhaling. "It's beautiful!"

"It's much prettier in full color," Prism said. And then, to Cressida's surprise, tears formed in Prism's eyes. "What if we can't find the missing rainbow, and I can never make art again?" she asked.

Cressida wrapped her arms around Prism's neck. "I promise to do my best to find the missing rainbow. When I'm worried about a problem, I always feel better when I get started finding a solution. So, why don't we go ahead and start searching?"

Prism sniffled as tears streamed down her face, smearing the fluorescent-green and violet paint on her cheeks. She took a deep breath and nodded.

"How about if you look over there?" Cressida said, pointing to the grass and trees on the other side of the river. "And I'll look over here." She pointed to a cluster of gnarled trees behind them. "And pretty soon, Sunbeam and Breeze will be here to help us."

"I'm still so worried we'll never find it,"

Prism said, her voice shaking a little. "But you're right. The best thing to do is get started looking." She took one more deep breath, blinked the tears from her eyes, and trotted toward the bridge.

Cressida walked toward the trees. She decided to start by climbing one of them and looking out over the valley to see if she could spot the rainbow. She chose the tallest tree, grabbed one of the branches, and began to hoist herself up.

"Who's there?" a low voice rumbled.

Surprised, Cressida let go of the tree branch and jumped back down to the ground. And that's when she saw that the tree's trunk held two large eyes, a nose that looked like a misshapen lump of clay, two ears that resembled pieces of cauliflower, and a mouth. The tree squinted at her and said, "Are you a Rainbow Cat? If you are, you most certainly can't climb me!"

Cressida giggled. "My name is Cressida Jenkins. I'm a human girl," she said. "I'm friends with Princess Prism, and I'm here to help find the missing rainbow."

The tree squinted at Cressida and slowly leaned toward her, so his trunk creaked and groaned. "I've always wanted to meet a human girl, and the truth is I can barely see you at all. You don't see my glasses, do you? When all the color disappeared, it was so windy my glasses blew off my face. Usually, I'd ask the Rainbow Cats to get them. But not after the fight we had this morning. I'm never speaking to those silly cats again."

Cressida scanned the ground and spotted a large pair of clear glasses on a bed of

see-through moss. She picked them up and slid them over the tree's eyes.

"You are a human girl!" he called out, laughing. "I'm Trevor, by the way. Trevor the Tree."

Cressida giggled again. "It's a pleasure to meet you, Trevor. You don't know, by any chance, where the missing rainbow might be, do you?" she asked.

"It's the strangest thing," Trevor said. "We trees saw it fly straight up into the air, right in front of us, not six feet away. But none of us saw where it landed. And believe me, we were looking."

"I was sure it would land in my branches, and I was all ready to catch it," the tree next to Trevor added. "But I haven't seen a glimmer of it. I'm Trina, by the way. And this is my son, Tristan." With one of her branches, Trina pointed to a shorter tree who looked much less gnarled.

"It's a pleasure to meet all three of you," Cressida said. Then she looked back at Trevor. "Would you mind if I climbed you?" she asked.

"Be my guest," he said.

As Cressida hoisted herself up from one branch to another, she couldn't help but ask, "Who are the Rainbow Cats?"

"The Rainbow Cats used to be our best friends," Trevor explained, sounding angry. "They scratched our trunks, which was wonderful because we trees get itchy, and there are lots of places we can't reach with our branches. In return, we let them perch and sleep on our branches."

Trina scoffed and sighed. "That was before this morning," she said, "when those silly cats had the nerve to claim that their paintings are more creative than ours. They kept meowing that ours are 'boring.'"

"Can you believe it?" Tristan interrupted. "Those Rainbow Cats are terrible painters. They don't have thumbs, so they can't even hold paintbrushes! All they do is smear paint and make paw prints!"

"Exactly!" Trevor agreed. "That's what I told them! And then I explained our paintings are better because not only do we have thumbs and fingers, but we each have several hands. I can hold fifteen paint-brushes at once! Trina can hold seventeen. Tristan can only hold eight, but he hasn't grown all his branches yet."

"I see," Cressida said, pulling herself up onto Trevor's highest branch. She wanted to be careful not to take sides. The argu-ment between the cats and the trees sounded like fights she had with Corey about who was better at bike riding or soc-cer. They were arguments that neither she nor Corey ever won, but they put both of them in a bad mood.

Cressida squinted as she scanned the Valley of Light for even the slightest glim-mer of color. But everything—every tree, every blade of grass, every flower, every turtle, every squirrel, every chipmunk, and every rock—looked clear and colorless. Where, she wondered, could the missing rainbow be? It seemed like it should be easy to spot. Worry that she might not be able to find the rainbow—and that Prism would be absolutely miserable without her ability to make art—swelled within Cressida. She took a deep breath. "It has to be somewhere," she whispered to herself. "I'll just have to keep looking."

Cressida quickly climbed back down Trevor. "It was wonderful to meet you," Cressida said to Trevor, Trina, and Tristan. "And if you'll excuse me, I'm going to keep looking for the missing rainbow."

"Good luck!" the trees called out.

Chapter Seven

Cressida walked beyond the trees and through a field of clear wild-flowers, scanning the ground for the rainbow and trying to imagine where else she could possibly look.

As Cressida carefully stepped over a clear turtle sunning herself on a see-through log, she heard a loud meow, followed by purring. She turned to her right and saw, slinking toward her, two large, see-through cats. Cressida grinned with excitement. After unicorns, cats were Cressida's favorite animal.

Cressida decided the cats were about the size of the leopards she had seen on a recent trip to the zoo on a school field trip. "Hello," one of the cats purred, flicking her tail. "You must be Cressida. I'm Riley. And this," Riley said, nodding to the other cat, "is my best friend, Roxy."

"Prism told us all about you," Roxy said, purring and rubbing her head against Cressida's shoulder. Cressida giggled as Roxy's long whiskers tickled her neck.

"Poor Prism is absolutely miserable," Riley added, pushing her head against Cressida's hand. Cressida scratched Riley between her ears, and the cat closed her eyes and purred loudly. Then Roxy flopped down and rolled onto her back. Keeping one hand on Riley's head, Cressida kneeled and rubbed Roxy's belly with her other hand. Roxy purred and extended her legs straight up into the air.

Though Cressida thought she could spend hours petting the two giant cats, she also knew she had better keep looking for the missing rainbow for Prism's sake. "I'm wondering," Cressida said, "if either of you know where the missing rainbow is."

"We both saw it go up into the air, right

in front of those awful trees," Roxy said. She curled her lips into a snarl and flicked her tail when she said the word "trees."

"But we didn't see it land," the two cats said in unison.

"We haven't seen it anywhere," Riley said. "And we've been walking around the Valley of Light all day looking for it."

"We even skipped two of our catnaps to search for it," Roxy added, yawning.

Cressida felt a pang of anxiety. But then she took a deep breath. There must, she thought, be somewhere she wasn't thinking to look. As she continued to scratch and pet the cats, she turned toward Trevor, Trina, and Tristan. She imagined the rainbow sailing straight up into the air in front of them. Then she looked up toward the sky to see if there was anywhere it might have landed on its way back down. But all she saw above the trees was a brilliant, cloudless, blue sky.

Deep in thought, Cressida stared into the distance. Her eyes caught sight of a gray rain cloud hanging low in the sky. For a moment, she watched it. And then she jumped up and down. "I have an idea!" she exclaimed, eyes wide with excitement. "I need to find Prism right away!"

"We'll take you to her," Riley said, stretching and crouching down. "Climb onto my back."

Cressida's heart raced. She was going to ride a giant cat! She grinned as she slid onto Riley's back and wrapped her arms around the cat's soft, furry neck.

"Off we go!" Riley purred, and then she and Roxy sprinted through the grass, leaped right over the river, and bounded over several large rocks. Cressida held on tight, her face pressed against Riley's fur, as the cat soared through the air.

"I had no idea you could jump so high," Cressida said.

"It's our specialty," Riley purred.

Soon, Cressida, Riley, and Roxy found Prism behind a large, clear bush talking to Breeze and Sunbeam. Tears rolled down Prism's cheeks, which were now completely clear. Her dandelion wreath lay in a withered ball by her hooves. "We'll never find it," she wailed. "I'll never be able to paint again."

"Oh Prism," Sunbeam said, "I promise we won't stop looking until we find it."

"But can you think of anywhere else to look?" Prism asked.

Sunbeam and Breeze shared a nervous glance. "Honestly," Breeze said, "I can't."

Prism cried harder. Sunbeam glared at

Breeze and whispered, "Stop being so honest!"

Breeze shrugged.

"I'm sorry to interrupt," Cressida said, "but I have one last idea. I'm not sure if it will work, but I think we should try it."

"I'll try anything!" Prism sniffled.

"The first thing we need to do," Cressida said, "is hurry over to the trees before that gray cloud in the distance stops raining." She pointed to the cloud.

Prism smiled even though tears still streamed down her face. "Your idea isn't from something you learned at that place you call school, is it?"

Cressida giggled. "As a matter of fact, it is," she said.

Prism kneeled so Cressida could climb onto her back. "Let's go!" Prism said, and with that, the three unicorns and the two cats sprinted toward the trees.

Chapter Eight

Cressida, Prism, Sunbeam, and Breeze stood just in front of Trevor, Trina, and Tristan. Riley and Roxy hung back and began to wash themselves, unwilling to make eye contact with the trees.

Cressida looked at Trevor. "You said the rainbow flew straight up from here, right?" she asked.

"Correct," Trevor said, nodding so his trunk creaked.

Cressida pointed to the rain cloud she had spotted in the distance and turned to Breeze. "Could you create a gust of wind that will bring that gray cloud right above us?"

Breeze frowned. "But then it will rain on us," she said.

"It's true we'll get a little wet," Cressida said. "But we'll dry off. And this might be our best chance to find the rainbow."

"Well, okay," said Breeze, sounding doubtful. She pointed her shiny blue horn at the rain cloud. The aquamarine on her ribbon necklace shimmered before a beam of light blue, glittery light shot from her horn. Suddenly, a comet-shaped gust of blue wind swirled upward and bolted toward the rain cloud. In a few seconds the rain cloud shot back toward them, the blue gust of wind pushing it forward.

For several seconds, the cloud hovered just over their heads, drizzling on Cressida and the three unicorns. Prism frowned as all the paint ran off her body and pooled in puddles around her hooves, leaving her clear once again. Sunbeam flattened her ears backward and said, "I hate getting wet." Breeze sighed and swished her tail impatiently. Cressida actually liked the feeling of the rain on her face and hair—it felt cool and refreshing.

When the rain lessened to just an

occasional drop, Cressida looked at Sun-beam. "Can you make the sun shine on us, as brightly as possible?"

"Gladly," said Sunbeam, flicking stringy, wet clumps of her yellow mane from her eyes. She pointed her horn toward the sun. The yellow sapphire on her chest glittered. A golden beam of glittery light shot from her horn. And then warm, bright sunlight shone down on Prism, Sunbeam, Breeze, and Cressida.

As the sunlight hit the thick, humid air, a rainbow appeared, dangling from the cloud. "There it is!" Cressida said, jump-ing up and down. "Now we need to get it before it disappears again!"

"Why would it disappear?" Prism asked,

looking confused. "Is this another thing you know about from school?"

Cressida giggled. "Yes! We had a science lesson in school where we learned that rainbows appear when the sun shines right after it rains. The reason is that even though we can't feel them, there are still raindrops hanging in the air, and each raindrop is like a prism. When the sun shines through the drops, a rainbow forms. The rainbow goes away when there aren't enough raindrops in the air anymore."

Sunbeam, Breeze, and Prism looked fascinated. "I always wondered where my name came from!" Prism exclaimed. "The more I hear about school, the more I want to go. Not only do you get to paint, but you also get to learn about prisms and rain-bows." Then Prism's face fell. "How are we going to get the rainbow? Even if you climb to the top of Trevor, you won't be able to reach it."

"I have an idea," Cressida said. "But the Rainbow Cats and the trees will have to work together."

"No way!" Trevor said.

"Absolutely not," Trina added.

Tristan crossed two branches across his trunk and grimaced.

Cressida took a deep breath. "I know you're angry at the Rainbow Cats," she said. "But I wonder if you might try talk-ing through your differences. Otherwise, Prism won't get her magic back. And you won't have your best friends to scratch your trunks."

Trevor, Trina, and Tristan glowered at the cats. But Trevor said, "You know, I admit my trunk has been awfully itchy today without the cats to scratch it."

Trina sighed. "My trunk is itchy, too," she said.

"Mine too," Tristan said, nodding.

Trevor looked down at his gnarled roots. "Well, I guess I'm willing to talk to the Rainbow Cats," he said.

Trina and Tristan nodded in agreement.

Cressida glanced at Riley and Roxy, who had stretched out in a particularly sunny patch of clear grass. Though they were pretending not to listen, Cressida could tell from their faces that they were paying attention.

"Well," Cressida said, feeling a little nervous, "I know you had an argument about whose artwork is better. And I bet you all feel hurt and angry. It makes sense to me that you'd also feel proud of your artwork, and the different ways you paint."

Riley and Roxy began to wash their faces. The trees frowned. "I think," Cressida said, "that the world would be an awfully boring place if everyone painted the same way. I'm glad there are many different styles and ways to paint. It's part of what makes looking at art, and making art, interesting. It's great that the trees paint by holding lots of different paintbrushes at once. And it's just as great that the cats use their paws to smear paint. Instead of arguing over whose artwork is better, maybe we could agree that your artwork is just different. And that those differences are wonderful."

The Rainbow Cats and the trees were silent. But Cressida noticed that the cats had stopped cleaning themselves. And the trees had thoughtful expressions on their faces. Finally, Trevor said, "I admit, it would be terribly boring if the only paintings in the Valley of Light were made by us trees." Trina and Tristan nodded.

Tristan looked at Riley and Roxy and said, "I thought those paintings you made last week with all the mice running on the rainbows were really neat. I never would have thought to paint that."

"Thank you," said Riley and Roxy.

"And we really liked those paintings you three trees made of your roots growing into the ground," Roxy added. "I never would have been able to come up with that idea."

"Thank you," the trees said in unison.

The Rainbow Cats and the trees looked at each other, but no one spoke. "Is there anything else you want to say to each other?" Cressida asked. "Sometimes, when I've had an argument with my brother or a friend, it helps us feel better if we say we're sorry. I always hate how I feel right before I apologize. But then I feel much better afterward."

Trina bit her lip. And then she said, "I'm sorry I said the trees are better at painting than the Rainbow Cats. I don't really believe that. I miss you, and I want to be friends again."

"Apology accepted," Riley said. "And I'm sorry I said the cats' paintings are better than the trees'. I only said that because I felt angry. I want to be friends again, too."

"I'm sorry, too," Trevor, Tristan, and Roxy all said at once. Then, they all laughed.

"Friends again?" Roxy asked.

"Most definitely friends again," Tristan responded. "And I'm wondering if one of you could scratch that place on my—" But before he could even finish his sentence, Roxy was sharpening her large, clear claws on the back of Tristan's trunk. He closed his eyes and grinned.

Cressida, Prism, Sunbeam, and Breeze exchanged looks of relief. "Good work, Cressida," Prism said.

Chapter Nine

Cressida looked up at the rainbow dangling from the gray cloud. She hoped she could get to it before it faded away. "Riley, could I ride you up to the top of Trevor? Then, if you jump as high and far as you can, I'll reach up and grab the rainbow."

"Absolutely!" Riley said. She crouched down, and Cressida swung her leg over the cat's back. "Up we go," Riley said, gripping Trevor's trunk with her claws. Cressida wrapped her arms around Riley's neck and squeezed Riley's back with her knees as Riley climbed up to the end of the highest branch.

"Get ready!" Riley called, springing forward into the air. As they soared through the sky, they passed right under the cloud. Cressida reached up and grabbed the rainbow. It felt soft and slippery in her hand, like a long silk scarf. As Cressida clung to the rainbow, Riley glided downward and landed gracefully on the ground.

"Thank you!" Cressida said, sliding off Riley.

"My pleasure!" Riley replied. Then she

slunk back over to Trevor, scaled his trunk once more, and lay down on one of his biggest branches. "I sure have missed my favorite perch today," she purred, yawning and closing her eyes.

Cressida spread out the rainbow on the ground. The ribbons of color shimmered, as though they were made of wet paint.

"Do you know what I'm supposed to do next?" Cressida asked the unicorns.

Sunbeam shrugged.

Breeze tilted her head to one side and said, "I have no idea."

"I guess they didn't teach you this part in school," Prism said.

Cressida laughed. "We'll just have to figure it out ourselves," she said, pulling the paintbrush from her smock pocket. It hummed and glowed in her hand. She touched the brush to the red stripe on the rainbow. Glittery light swirled around her as the paintbrush filled with red. Cressida touched the bristles to the ground, and five blades of grass turned from clear to a bright, vibrant red. Next, she tapped the brush against Trevor. A swirl of red flowered on his otherwise clear bark.

Cressida smiled with delight. But then she heard a sniffling noise. She turned and saw tears streaming down Prism's face.

"What's wrong?" Cressida asked, surprised her unicorn friend wasn't thrilled to see color returning to the Valley of Light.

"I'm glad and grateful you found the

rainbow," Prism sniffled, "but at this rate, it will take weeks to repaint the whole valley."

Breeze furrowed her brow. "I'd offer to help, but I don't even have a paintbrush."

"If we're going to be here for a long time, maybe I should go get some snacks," suggested Sunbeam.

Cressida paused. Prism was right that if Cressida repainted the Valley of Light all by herself, it might take weeks—and maybe even months—to restore the valley's colors. What they needed, Cressida thought, were more painters. And that's when she remembered Titania's offer to help. "Prism," Cressida said, "would you ask Titania if she and the fairies might be willing to come help paint?"

Before Prism could respond, a familiar voice behind Cressida and the unicorns said, "Of course we would!"

Cressida turned and saw Titania fluttering her wings and holding a giant paintbrush. Behind her hovered more fairies than Cressida could count, each holding a paintbrush as they beat their wings. "We felt a huge gust of wind—so strong it could only have come from Princess Breeze— and then we saw the rainbow hanging from a rain cloud in the distance. That's when we all grabbed our paintbrushes and rushed over to you. Nothing would make us happier than to help paint the Valley of Light."

A grin spread across Prism's face. "Thank you," she said.

Titania turned to the fairies behind her. "Fill up your paintbrushes!" she called out.

The fairies cheered and laughed as they fluttered over to the rainbow and touched their brushes to the ribbons of red, orange, yellow, green, blue, and purple. Their brushes hummed as the fairies then spread out across the valley and began to paint.

Soon, violet and lemon-yellow wildflowers swayed in the wind. Red, orange, yellow, green, blue, and purple stripes cascaded down the Rainbow Cats' backs. They looked, Cressida realized, just like

the cat on her shirt. Curly red, turquoise, magenta, and mint-green lines danced up the trees' trunks. Fuchsia and maroon fish leaped from swirls of mustard-yellow and light orange river water. Blades of grass in every color Cressida could imagine shimmered in the sunlight.

Cressida looked over at Prism, who was still completely see-through. Though the unicorn looked thrilled and relieved to see the color returning so rapidly to the Valley of Light, Cressida could tell her friend felt anxious to have her magic working again. "Would you like me to paint you and your amethyst now?" Cressida asked.

"Yes!" cried Prism, dancing with excitement. "I can't wait to be back in my very own purple coat, with a magic gemstone that actually works!"

"I bet!" Cressida said, dipping her paintbrush into the rainbow's purple stripe and touching the bristles to Prism. Soon, Prism's coat was a glossy lavender, her mane and tail shone like purple silk, her horn and hooves glimmered like purple foil. Cressida pressed her paintbrush against Prism's gemstone. Purple glittery light swirled around the amethyst, and then it shimmered a vibrant purple.

"Marvelous!" Titania exclaimed, admiring Cressida's work. And then the fairy queen dipped her brush into the rainbow's green stripe and painted Prism's ribbon.

"I have my magic back!" Prism sang as she danced in a circle. "Now I can make art again! Does anyone have any paper?"

"I do!" said Roxy, and she darted away and returned with a large, blank piece of paper in her mouth. She put it down in a patch of green, orange, and purple moss in front of Prism.

"Thank you!" Prism said.

Next, the unicorn pointed her horn toward the paper. Her amethyst shimmered. And then a beam of glittery purple light shot from her horn. Suddenly, a blob that included every color of the rainbow appeared on the paper. It looked, Cressida thought, a little bit like a rainbow puddle. Prism kept shooting purple light at the paper, and Cressida watched as the blob slowly took the shape of a human. By the time Prism was done, Cressida realized she had just painted a girl with bright red hair, green skin, purple eyes, blue ears, and a yellow nose.

"It's you!" Prism said. "Do you like it?"

"I love it!" Cressida said.

"I've been wanting to paint you ever since you told me you painted a picture of me!" Prism said. "Maybe you could even take it home with you?"

"Really?" Cressida asked, imagining putting the picture up on the wall of her room, right next to the pictures of Sunbeam, Flash, Bloom, and Prism.

"It's my gift to you," Prism said. "Thank you for helping to restore all the color to the Valley of Light and for getting my magic back. I love creating art more than anything else in the whole world, and it was miserable not to be able to do what I love."

"Thank you so very much," Cressida said. She pulled the paper off the mossy ground, rolled it up, and put it in her back pocket.

"I know you probably need to get home," Prism said, "but I'm so glad you could see the Valley of Light in full color."

"Me too," Cressida said, and she put her arm around Prism. "And I want you to know that I don't think your purple coat is boring at all. I'm glad to see you looking like yourself again."

"Well, thank you," Prism said, blushing.

"I agree," Breeze said. "I like you just the way you are. And I bet you're relieved you can make art again."

"I sure am," Prism said.

Just then, Cressida's stomach growled. And she thought about her math homework, still in her backpack. "I've had so much fun today," Cressida said, "but I think I'd better get home. I can't wait to put your painting up on my bedroom wall. And I'm ready to get started on my homework."

"Homework?" Prism said, looking confused. "Is that something else related to school?"

"It sure is," Cressida said.

Prism smiled and nodded. "Well, I don't know what we'd do without you, Cressida," she said. "Please come back soon."

"Yes," said Breeze, "please do."

"I promise I will," Cressida said. And she pulled the magic, old-fashioned key out of her pocket and said, "Take me home, please."

Immediately, the Valley of Light began to spin into a rainbow-colored blur before everything went pitch black. Cressida felt the wonderful sensation of flying straight up into the air. She giggled. Soon, she found herself sitting on the forest floor, under the oak tree with the magic keyhole. For a moment, the woods spun. And then, everything was still.

Cressida smiled. She stood and looked down. Her rainbow smock and the magic paintbrush were gone, and her sneakers were silver again. She touched her head. The dandelion wreath was gone, too. But she felt something in her back pocket: the rolled-up picture of her that Prism had painted. She touched it and smiled, eager to hang it next to the other paintings on her bedroom wall. And then she skipped home, the pink lights on her sneakers blinking merrily.

DON'T MISS OUR NEXT MAGICAL ADVENTURE!

TURN THE PAGE FOR A SNEAK PEEK . . .

In the top tower of Spiral Palace, Ernest the wizard-lizard stared at his bookshelf. He tilted his scaly green head to one side and his pointy hat almost toppled off. "Hmm," he said. "What book of spells should I study next? *Magic Storms and Other Bewitched Weather*? No, the unicorn princesses wouldn't like that much. *Enchanted Bangs and Conjured Crashes*? Nope, too loud. What about—"

Before he could finish his sentence, a loud thumping on the door interrupted him. "Come in!" he called out, straightening his hat and cloak.

The wooden door creaked open, and a red dragon wearing a white chef's hat and apron entered. "Good morning, Ernest!" the dragon boomed. His flame-colored eyes glimmered, and blue smoke puffed from his nostrils. In one clawed hand he held eight bulbs of garlic.

"Hello, Drew," Ernest said, smiling eagerly. "Can I help you with something?"

"You sure can!" Drew bellowed. "We dragons down in the palace kitchen were wondering if you might provide us with some magical assistance."

"With pleasure!" Ernest said, jumping with glee.

"Fantastic," Drew said as threads of smoke rose from his nose. "Could you turn these bulbs of garlic into eight large cooking vats? We're preparing to make the Blast Feast for Princess Breeze, but none of our usual pots are big enough."

"I know just the right book of spells!" Ernest exclaimed. He grabbed a thin, red book entitled *Magic in the Kitchen* and flipped to a page that said, in large letters across the top, "Big Pots, Large Pans, Giant Vats, and Humungous Cauldrons."

"Thank you!" Drew said, and he set the garlic bulbs down on Ernest's table.

"I'm sure I can do this one perfectly on the first try," Ernest said. He read over the spell several times, mouthing the words silently. Then he stepped up to his table, grabbed his magic wand from his cloak pocket, and lifted it into the air. He took a deep breath before he chanted, "Cookily Slookily Stockily Stew! Garlic Starlic Smarlic Smew! Make Eight Bats for a Tasty Brew!"

Ernest waited. The bulbs of garlic didn't spin or jump or quiver. Instead, thunder rumbled. Ernest scratched his head. "Oh

Emily Bliss lives just down the street from a forest. From her living room window, she can see a big oak tree with a magic keyhole. Like Cressida Jenkins, she knows that unicorns are real.

Sydney Hanson was raised in Minnesota alongside numerous pets and brothers. She has worked for several animation shops, including Nickelodeon and Disney Interactive. In her spare time she enjoys traveling and spending time outside with her adopted brother, a Labrador retriever named Cash. She lives in Los Angeles.

www.sydwiki.tumblr.com

dear," Ernest said. "I'm not sure why that didn't work."

"Well," Drew said, "I'm not a wizard, so I don't know for sure, but I think it's because you said 'bats' instead of 'vats.'"

"Oh dear!" Ernest said again, slapping his hand to his forehead. Ernest turned and looked out the window just as eight bolts of silver lightning tore through the sky right above a distant meadow.